Dudley's Muddley Day

Lib

JOSH wEBB

Illustrated by Gabriele Antonini

Thanks to Patricia Posner

EGMONT

We bring stories to life

Book Band: Purple

First published in Great Britain 2011
by Egmont UK Ltd
239 Kensington High Street, London W8 6SA
Text and illustrations copyright © Egmont UK Ltd 2011
ISBN 978 1 4052 5948 4
10 9 8 7 6 5 4 3 2 1
A CIP catalogue record for this title is available from the British Library.
Printed in Singapore.

Contents

Red Bananas

Come and meet some animal friends,
You'll have fun in this crazy place,

There are trees, logs and rocks and a water
hollow – where the hippos love to wallow.
Dens and burrows, lakes and lairs – have a
look for sleepy bears. Holes and ponds and
muddy places – where elephants go to clean

they're all shapes and sizes.
there are lots of funny surprises!

their faces. Lots of plants and grassland, too –
whoops there goes a kangaroo! There's a
marsh and a swamp – with a crocodile in –
and near the edge of the swamp is a terrapin.

Worrying News

'Dudley. Dudley! I can't get out.'

Dudley the terrapin opened his eyes and looked around. 'I thought I heard somebody calling me,' he said. 'It's not Frank Crocodile. Frank's gone for a swim. Poppy is over there. But it couldn't have been Poppy calling me. She's too busy preening her feathers. I can't see anyone else.'

Dudley shook his head. 'Maybe I was dreaming,' he said. He closed his eyes and went back to sleep.

'Dudley. Dudley! Please let me out.'

Dudley opened his eyes and looked around.
He saw buttercups and daisies and some
clumps of tall grass. But he still couldn't see
who was talking to him.

'How peculiar,' he said, feeling puzzled.

When Dudley felt puzzled he always scratched his head. He lifted one foot and, as he started to scratch . . .

A worm popped up out of the ground. 'Phew! I'm so glad you moved your foot, Dudley. I couldn't get out of my tunnel.'

'Oh, Oscar, it was you I could hear talking,' said Dudley. 'I'm sorry, I didn't know my foot was over your tunnel.'

'That's all right,' said Oscar. He wriggled more of his body out of the little hole. 'Listen, I've got something to tell you. It's about Joe. The poor bear cub is under the weather. He feels too miserable to move.'

Poor Joe!

Just then, Iris and Jack, the butterflies, flew down and landed on Dudley's nose.

'Has Oscar told you the news?' they said. 'Joe is under the weather.'

'It isn't nice being under the weather,' said Oscar.

Iris fluttered her wings. 'It isn't. And it might be catching,' she said.

'Oh, dear,' thought Dudley. 'Perhaps big, grey rain clouds might come over me too.'

'We'll go and spread the news,' said Iris and Jack, flying away.

Come on, Jack!

'So will I,' said Oscar. He wriggled down into his tunnel.

Dudley was worried about grey clouds.

But even when he'd tucked himself inside his shell, Dudley kept thinking about the worrying news.

Dudley's Good Idea

After a while, Dudley felt the ground tremble a bit. That didn't scare him. He knew it must be Minnie the elephant.

'Trump-trump,' said Minnie. She wiggled her trunk under Dudley's shell and picked him up.

Dudley peeked out. 'Hello, Minnie,' he said. 'Have you heard about Joe?'

'I have,' said Minnie. 'He's feeling miserable because he's under the weather. The poor little bear won't move from his lair. Maybe we should go and see him. We could try to cheer him up.'

'Iris said it might be catching,' Dudley said. 'I don't want grey clouds over me.'

'I don't, either,' Minnie agreed. 'But it might not happen to us.'

Dudley put one toe in his mouth and nibbled it. Dudley often did that when he wanted to get an idea.

After a while, he nodded his head.

'Have you got an idea?' asked Minnie.

'Yes,' said Dudley. 'Let's go to the Umbrella Tree and see if there's a *real* umbrella hanging on its branches.'

'Why?' asked Minnie.

'We could take it for Joe,' said Dudley.

'He might feel better if he can hide from the weather. I can pull my head, legs and tail inside my shell. That always hides me very well. But Joe hasn't got a shell to hide in. He can shelter under the umbrella instead.'

'That's a good idea,' said Minnie.

They set off along the twisty track. Minnie walked on tippy-toes so she wouldn't tread on Dudley.

They went past some fir trees and crunchy-crunched their way over the pine cones on the ground. Then, at last, they came to the Umbrella Tree.

'Trump-trump,' said Minnie. 'There *is* a real umbrella!' She curled her trunk around the umbrella's handle and lifted the umbrella down.

'Hooray!' said Dudley.

The two friends set off again.

Found one!

Grumpy Ella

Minnie and Dudley had only walked a little way when they heard a fluttering and a mutter-mutter-muttering.

'It must be grumpy Ella,' said Minnie, looking up into the trees. 'She's the only parrot who mutter-mutter-mutters like that.'

Dudley stretched his head and neck upwards, looking for Ella. 'Good morning, Ella,' he called.

'Dismal day. Dismal day,' Ella said as she flew down. 'Have you heard about Joe? He's under the weather.'

'We're going to see him,' said Minnie. 'To try and cheer him up.'

'We're taking him this umbrella,' said Dudley.

Ella squawked. 'Umbrella! Umbrella! How will that cheer him up? It doesn't make me feel cheerful.'

Umbrella!

'He can shelter from the rain clouds underneath it,' said Dudley.

'It doesn't look very big,' said Ella. 'Dismal, dismal day. We'll all have to get under the umbrella. All squashed up together. Hiding from the horrid weather.'

'Oh, dear,' said Dudley. He started to worry about the rain cloud again.

'Trump-trump,' said Minnie. 'It's my turn to get a good idea now. Let's go to the Sunshine Tree and see if there are any *real* sunglasses hanging on its branches.'

'Why?' asked Dudley.

'Because when the horrid weather has gone, the sun will come out,' said Minnie. 'Joe will need some sunglasses then.'

'Sun! Sun!' squawked Ella. 'We might get

sunburn. I'm going back to sit on my branch.'

So Ella flew off and Minnie and Dudley walked on. They went past a lake and then through some long grass. At last, they came to the Sunshine Tree.

There were some sunglasses hanging on a low branch. Dudley scrambled on to Minnie's foot and managed to reach them.

There are some sunglasses!

23

'You better let me carry them,' said Minnie.
Then the two friends set off again.

They hadn't walked far when they heard a
fluttering and a mutter-mutter-muttering.

'I'll come with you to Joe Bear's lair. You'll
have to tell me when we get there. I got some
sunglasses and now I can't see where I'm
going. But I won't get sunburn if the sun comes
along when the weather has gone.'

Dudley smiled at Ella, who looked very silly.

A Shock for Dudley

'Minnie,' said Dudley after they'd walked up a big hill and down the other side, 'could we stop for a little rest? My legs are tired.'

'I heard that,' said Ella. 'Dismal day. We'll never get there if you keep stopping.'

'I only need a little rest,' Dudley said. 'I'll clamber up on to that rock.'

Dudley liked resting on top of rocks. He settled down happily. But suddenly . . .

'Oh, dear,' he said. 'I feel water underneath my chin. The rain cloud must have fallen and turned upside down.

I'm over the weather!'

'Is that you, Dudley? It's Leo, here. You
aren't over the weather. You're over my
hollow. I'm splashing around in the mud.'

'That's all right, then,' said Dudley. He
wriggled to the edge of the rock and peered

Hello, Leo!

downwards. He could see Leo the hippo having a wonderful time sploshing and bouncing around in gooey wet mud and water.

'It isn't all right at all,' Ella grumbled as she flew towards Leo's hollow.

'Hippos are meant to wallow in a hollow,' she said. 'Not splash mud everywhere.'

Leo laughed and splashed harder. Ella got covered in mud. 'Parrots are meant to have bright feathers. Not mud-coloured ones,' said Leo.

'That was a bit naughty of you, Leo,' said Minnie, smiling.

Then she laughed, too, when Leo splashed mud all over her.

'The umbrella and sunglasses are muddy as well,' said Dudley. 'You can wash them in this clean puddle, Minnie.'

'Why have you got them?' asked Leo.

'They're for Joe,' said Minnie, dipping the sunglasses in the puddle. 'We're on our way to see him. We want to cheer him up. He's under the weather.'

'Poor Joe,' said Leo. 'I'll come with you. What sort of weather is he under? A rain cloud, or a hailstone cloud?'

'Oh dear,' said the terrapin.

'I don't like hailstones. They make a terrible noise pinging and dinging on my shell.'

'We don't know what sort of weather Joe is under,' said Minnie.

'He might be under a snow cloud,' said Leo. 'He'll feel cold if he is. The Mitten Tree is just over there. Let's go and see if there are any real mittens hanging on its branches. We'll take him a scarf as well. A scarf will be good if it snows.'

'Oh, no. Not snow,' said Ella.

Leo found a scarf. Minnie and Dudley walked over to the Mitten Tree. There were

30

a lot of real mittens hanging on the branches.

'Joe's favourite colour is orange,' said Dudley.

Minnie took two orange mittens off the tree.

Got some!

'Mittens! Mittens!' said Ella. 'They won't stop snow from freezing my feathers. I think I'll fly back to my branch.'

Ella couldn't see where she was going. She flew round and round in circles.

'If there's lots of weather, there might be a rainbow,' said Minnie.

There was a fluttering and a mutter-mutter-muttering. 'I heard that,' said Ella. 'I'll come with you after all. I like rainbows. Why didn't you tell me there might be a rainbow? Are we nearly there yet?'

'Count up to one hundred and then we'll be there,' said Minnie. 'Elephant-one, elephant-two, elephant-three . . .'

Dudley giggled as he walked slowly along with Minnie and Leo. Leo bounced every time he said a number. And every time Leo bounced a bit more mud dropped off him.

'He'll be nice and clean by the time we get to Joe's lair!' thought Dudley.

A Tale of Woe

The friends had just got to number elephant-ninety-seven, when Dudley started to giggle again. 'Look at those tall wellies outside Joe's lair,' he said. 'Somebody must have left them there for Joe. But they'll be much too long for him.'

'You are silly, Dudley,' said Ella. 'The wellies belong to Ava the giraffe. She's wearing them.'

'Oh,' said Dudley. 'Ava is too high up for me to see her.'

Hi!

He stretched out his
neck as far as he could.
'Hello up there, Ava,' he
called. 'Have you come to see
Joe as well?'

'Not really,' Ava said. 'I don't
know what all the fuss is about.
He's had friends coming to see him
all day.'

'Joe is under the weather,' said Minnie.

'Well, I feel under the weather, too, you
know,' said Ava.

'But I can't see a cloud over you,' said Leo.

'No, I can't either,' said Minnie.

'I've got a stiff neck . . . a pimple on my tongue . . . my feet hurt . . . my legs itch . . . there's a pain in my tail and my throat is sore,' said Ava. She bent her head down so that the friends could see she looked ill.

'What's all that got to do with the weather?' asked Dudley. 'And where is your cloud?'

Ava groaned. 'Now I'm getting a headache with all these questions,' she said.

'It's a dismal day, Ava,' said Ella, flying down. 'My feathers feel stiff because Leo splashed them with muddy water. And . . .'

'Come on,' whispered Minnie to Leo and Dudley. 'Let's leave these two to grumble together and we'll go and find Joe.'

Where is Joe Bear?

Joe Bear wasn't in his lair. The friends were puzzled. Then they saw him in his garden, leaning back against a log pillow.

'Look! There isn't any weather over Joe, either,' said Leo.

'Hi, Joe! Has your weather cloud gone then?' asked Dudley.

'What are you talking about?' Joe asked, looking puzzled.

'We heard you were under the weather,' said Dudley.

'That doesn't mean I've got a weather cloud over me,' said Joe. 'It just means I don't feel very well.'

'Oh, dear!' said Dudley. 'We made a big mistake. I feel silly now.'

Oops!

'So do I!' Minnie said, blushing.

'Not being well makes me feel miserable,' said Joe.

I feel ill.

'Poor Joe,' Minnie said. 'Shall we play a nice quiet game to cheer you up?'

'Let's tell him stories about the things we brought for him,' said Dudley.

'Good idea,' Leo said.

'Once upon this morning, we thought you were under a grey cloud,' said Dudley. 'So we decided to bring you something special. You see, I can hide inside my shell.'

Dudley's head, legs and tail disappeared. 'Like this. My shell always hides me very well from bad weather,' said Dudley in a muffled voice.

Then Dudley popped his head back out.
'But you haven't got a shell, Joe.'

'That's right, I haven't,' said Joe.

'So we went to the Umbrella Tree to see
if there was a real umbrella hanging on its
branches,' said Dudley. 'There was. And we
brought it so you could hide under it from the
weather cloud.'

Dudley gave the umbrella
to Joe.

Joe smiled and
put the
umbrella up.

Thank you!

'Twice upon this morning, we thought when the weather cloud had gone, the sun might come along,' said Minnie. 'So we went to the Sunshine Tree and we saw this pair of sunglasses hanging on its branches.'

Minnie gave the sunglasses to Joe.

Joe smiled and put the sunglasses on.

Leo bounded around. 'My turn now,' he said. 'Three upon this morning, we thought you might be under a snow cloud. So we found these mittens on the Mitten Tree.'

Leo put the mittens on Joe. 'The End,' Leo said with a smile.

Joe started to laugh really, really hard. 'I feel much better after hearing those stories,' he gasped.

'That's all right then,' said Dudley, giggling at Joe. 'You look funny under the umbrella wearing all the things we brought,' he said.

'It's funny that you got the wrong end of the stick,' said Joe.

'Stick?' said Dudley. 'What stick? We didn't bring a stick. Do you want me to find you one, Joe?'

'Oh heck,' said Joe. 'Don't make me laugh

Oh, Dudley!

again. I'll get tummy ache. Getting the wrong end of the stick just means you got things a bit wrong, Dudley.'

'Oh, dear,' said Dudley. 'That's twice this morning I've got things wrong. What a muddley day!'

'We've had a good time, though,' said
Minnie. She put her trunk around Dudley and
gave him a hug.

'Yes, Dudley's muddley day was the best
time ever,' said Leo, bouncing around.

Dudley smiled at his friends. 'I hope we have
another muddley day soon,' he thought. 'And
maybe another elephant hug, too!'